HOSTAGE

Darren G. Burton

CHAPTER ONE

Tyler had no idea where he was. Everything was a blank. His last memory had been closing up his restaurant and preparing to go home.

He'd been in the alley out the back smoking a cigarette. That was when a van had pulled up and four men with guns had got out. At first he'd thought it was some sort of police raid, only the guys hadn't been dressed in the uniform of the PNP or NBI, and looked more like they were from the provinces rather than belonging to a government department.

Even though he'd been in the Philippines for years, and knew a few words of the local dialect, he still didn't understand the language and had no idea what the men were saying to each other as they'd approached him, four guns pointed at his midsection. One of the men had lowered his gun and fished something from his pocket. With his teeth he'd pulled off a cap and stuck a syringe into Tyler's arm before he'd had a chance to react.

Everything had gone hazy very rapidly after that, and next thing he knew we was groggily waking up in a small room on a cement floor, his head aching and a sour taste in his mouth.

He had no clue how long he'd been out. It could have been an hour. It could have been days. All he knew was that it was dark out, a fact made obvious by the black sky he could see through a small open window with rusted bars on it.

The room was hot and humid and his skin and clothing felt damp and clammy with sweat. There was no fan in the room that he could make out in the gloom, and certainly no air conditioning.

In fact, there was nothing in the room except him. On the opposite wall was the entrance door. He staggered to his feet and made his way over to it, but when he tried the handle he soon discovered it was locked.

No real surprises there, he thought.

Tyler put his ear to the door, but couldn't hear any sounds coming from the other side. He went over to the window then and looked outside, but all he saw was jungle in the darkness. Lightning licked across the sky far off in the distance, too far away to hear any thunder or light up the scene.

He rummaged in his pockets and found he still had his cigarettes. He lit one and puffed on it tenaciously as he continued to stare out into the night.

Who were these four armed men who'd.....well, kidnapped him basically? He had no enemies. What could they possibly want with him? Was it a case of mistaken identity? He hoped that's all it was, and when they realized their mistake, they would set him free and send him home.

But then again, maybe they wouldn't. They hadn't been wearing masks. He'd seen their faces, even though it was all a bit of a blur. They might fear he'd identify them and turn them in to the authorities.

Would he do that if they set him free? He wasn't sure. All he was certain about was wanting to get out of there.

The effects of whatever they'd jabbed him with to knock him out had pretty much worn off now. He was feeling awake and alert, and the more lucid his mind became, the more his heart clenched with fear of what was to come.

CHAPTER TWO

Dan Mason stared out the window of the A320 Airbus as it flew over the many thousands of islands that made up the Philippines. After a long flight from Los Angeles to Hong Kong, it had been a brief layover until the connecting flight to Cebu; the Philippines' second largest city.

The sun was setting as the aircraft lost altitude in preparation for landing at Mactan-Cebu International Airport. Twenty minutes later, when the jet's wheels kissed the tarmac with a squeal, twilight had descended over the city.

Keen to get off the plane, Dan was one of the first to his feet when the fasten seat belt light eventually went off. He reached into the overhead compartment and withdrew a small backpack, then stood there in the crush and impatiently waited for the doors to open and the people lined up ahead of him to disembark.

After what seemed like an eternity, he was finally off the plane and walking through the terminal building, where he negotiated Immigration and followed the crowd to the luggage carousel. Once outside, a taxi took him to his hotel in Cebu city and, being peak hour, it was a short journey that took a hell of a long time. He'd never quite seen traffic like this place, yet he'd heard it was nowhere near as bad as Manila, the nation's capital.

The words "organized chaos" entered his mind as the taxi

attempted to weave through the bottleneck by any route possible.

It was well and truly full dark by the time he reached his hotel in the center of Cebu, checked in and was shown to his room. The bellhop departed with a tip, leaving Dan alone to settle in.

The room was standard hotel fare, with a double bed, flat screen TV, desk area, small bar fridge and a bathroom. It was clean and tidy enough. Most likely he wouldn't be spending much time in the room anyway.

He checked his watch and figured he had time for a quick shower and change of clothes before going to his friend's house for a late dinner and a very important chat.

Half an hour later Dan was back in a taxi and motoring towards a destination southwest of the city center. Traffic had mercifully thinned out a little since earlier and the going was definitely faster. When he arrived at a two storey home nestled into the foothills of the mountains in the west, he paid the cab driver and got out.

A concrete fence topped with spikes of metal surrounded the home, obviously designed to keep undesirable company out. Dan glanced left and right along the street. There weren't many people about, but there was some sort of small, ramshackle store down the road and a few young men were out the front drinking liquor and smoking cigarettes. Two stray dogs went running past, paying Dan no attention whatsoever.

Even after dark the air was hot and humid, and he felt sweat beading on his brow as he pressed a buzzer on the outside of a steel gate. A moment later an exterior light came on, the front door opened and a tall man strolled out to meet him. Dan and the man shook hands once the gate was unlocked and Dan followed his friend into the house.

"It's been a while," Dan said. He hadn't seen his friend John Harvard for some time.

"At least a few years," John replied.

"I've always been meaning to visit you out here. I always planned to be a tourist though, when I got here."

John shrugged as they stepped in through the front door. "If everything turns out well, maybe that can come later?"

While he and John had caught up a few times when John had returned to the United States for visits, Dan had yet to meet his Filipino wife. Tonight would be the first time.

Two young kids, a boy and a girl, raced out to meet their guest. In turn, each of them grabbed Dan's hand and touched it to their forehead. Dan smiled at the kids and then looked quizzically at John.

"It's a sign of respect to their elders," John explained. "Part of Filipino culture."

"Nice. How old are they?"

"William is eight and Angel just turned five a few weeks back."

Inside the house several air conditioners were running. It wasn't super cool, but definitely a lot better than the sticky heat outdoors. Dan was led through into a dining area, where the table was laid out with an assortment of food, most of which he didn't recognize.

A very short and petite woman appeared from the kitchen carrying a large bowl of rice. Next to John's tall frame she looked tiny.

When she'd placed the rice on the table, John introduced his wife to Dan. "This is Joy, my asawa. That means 'wife' in the Filipino language. It can also mean 'husband'."

Dan shook hands with Joy. "Nice to finally meet you." He figured she was in her thirties, but looked young for her age. She was very attractive and looked to be a mix of several Asian cultures, and possibly a touch of Spanish as well.

John was fidgeting around and looking agitated. "Let's eat, and then we can talk more about what's going on."

It was the first time Dan had dined on authentic Filipino food and it was an interesting experience. Some he liked and some he wasn't so fussed on, but he tried everything and did his best to enjoy the meal, occasionally tossing compliments in Joy's direction.

When dinner was done, everyone pitched in to clean up and wash up, then John and Dan settled in the living room to talk, armed with some local beers.

"Tell me again everything you know, from the beginning," Dan said.

Before flying out to the Philippines from his home in Miami, Dan had received a call from John about a family problem. Dan knew a little about it, but chances were there had been further developments while he was in transit.

John sucked in a deep breath and took a swig of beer before he spoke. "It's been four days since my younger brother disappeared from outside his restaurant. As you know I thought kidnapping was one possibility at the time, but it's since been confirmed."

Dan leaned forward in his seat. "Confirmed how?"

John seemed to study the label on his beer bottle a moment before answering. He looked into Dan's eyes. "With a ransom demand."

"So someone called you?"

John nodded. "Last night I got a call from a man who refused to identify himself. The number was blocked as well. No way of telling if it was a landline or cell phone. He spoke English well enough, but I could tell he was a Filipino. He said if I wanted Tyler back alive, I would need to pay a ransom of five million US dollars."

"Five million!" Dan exclaimed and took a long pull on his beer.

"I know. As if I have that kind of money."

"Did they also contact the police with their demands? Or the government?" Dan wanted to know.

John shook his head. "Not as far as I know. I called the NBI agent who's leading up the investigation into Tyler's disappearance and informed him of the call and ransom demand. The NBI is like the FBI in the States. He hadn't received any such calls and wasn't aware of any other government department getting a call from the kidnappers either. He also suggested I don't pay any ransom. And to keep him in the loop."

"And what do you think about that? I know you don't have five million, but we all know what happens to people if some sort of ransom isn't paid to these nutcases."

"We don't even know who has Tyler yet. They haven't

identified themselves. We don't know if it's some extremist terrorist group like Abu Sayyaf. That mob don't normally abduct people from places like Cebu city. It's usually down in Mindanao or somewhere in the Sulu Sea." John shrugged and looked at the floor. "But if it is them, then we all know Tyler's life is in grave danger if I don't pay them something."

"Did they state how they want you to pay the ransom? Bank account transfer? Cash drop off?"

John shook his head. "Not yet. They said they would call me again soon. The way I understand it is you usually need to enlist some sort of local negotiator to broker the deal and arrange the release of a hostage." He looked at Dan again. "I don't really know what you can do. I know you're not a local and it's your first time here, but I felt I needed to call in help from somebody I trust, somebody not from here. I also thought your detective background might come in handy."

Dan nodded his understanding. Until a few years ago he'd a been a detective first grade for the Miami PD, before venturing out into his own freelance business; which was really a mix of private investigator, troubleshooter and mercenary, among other things.

"So the official investigation. How's that going?" Dan asked.

John's face clouded over. "It's not going, really. That's another reason why I called you. The local authorities seem very blase about the whole thing. Maybe they have so many other things to deal with that one missing foreigner isn't really a top priority." He finished his beer and cracked open another one. "Despite some recent changes, corruption is still rampant in this country too. You never really know who you can trust and who's on the take."

John's wife entered the room then, cradling a glass of red wine between her hands. Joy took up a position on the couch next to her husband. She smiled at Dan a little nervously, then placed a hand on John's thigh.

"The kid's are in their room playing games on their iPads."

John nodded, sipped some beer.

Joy looked at Dan with her deep brown eyes. "You were friends with John in the Marines?"

"That's how we first met," Dan said. "Only John managed to finish his training, whereas I had to quit due to a serious knee injury." He unconsciously massaged his right knee. "It still gives me problems sometimes." He recalled the trouble it had been giving him on his last assignment on Purgatory Island.

"We always remained friends and stayed in touch, though," John added. "Which is why Dan's here now. I need his help with this."

"Your brother's married to a Filipina too, isn't he?" Dan quizzed.

John nodded again. "He's been married for four years and been living here most of that time. His wife's name is Larissa."

"Where is Larissa now? Do they have any kids?"

"No kids." It was joy who answered.

"Larissa's been too afraid to be at home since my brother disappeared. She's worried the kidnappers might come for her next. She's staying with family here in Cebu."

"And what does she know about Tyler's abduction?" Dan wanted to know. "Does she have any helpful information?"

John shook his head. "She knows about as much as we do. All Larissa knows is that Tyler never came home from the restaurant he owns. And now it's been confirmed that it's a kidnapping for ransom."

"Did the kidnappers contact Larissa with ransom demands?"

"I don't think so," John said with a frown. "She never mentioned getting a call from them. I guess they figure I'm the one with all the money. A foreigner. The older brother. You know."

Dan thought for a moment. "Are Tyler and his wife close?"

John answered without hesitation. "Sure. They seem just as close as Joy and I are." Joy smiled and squeezed his thigh in response to his words.

"Does your brother have a lot of money? Is there any reason for anyone to target him in particular?"

"None that we can think of," said John. "Often these kidnappings are pretty random. The kidnappers, whether it be Abu Sayyaf or some other mob, don't always target the wealthy, or even foreigners."

"So earlier, when you said they've given you no details about the ransom payment other than the amount, I assume they haven't yet given you any sort of deadline to pay it?"

"No, not yet."

"When they do, maybe you should offer them something. It might at least buy us some time to figure out who they are and where they've got Tyler holed up."

John nodded. "I was kinda thinking the same thing. Best case scenario is they'll release him if I pay them something. Bad for business if they don't."

"What do you think you can offer?"

Dan opened another beer and looked at his friend expectantly.

"We've got a few businesses here doing quite well by local standards, plus some money saved from my days in the Corps." He fell silent, doing some mental calculations, then eventually shrugged. "I don't know, maybe about fifty grand. I know that's a far cry from five million, but it's all I've got to spare."

Dan sipped some beer. "I've heard of amounts like that doing the trick before and getting people freed. Often these groups of crazies just want to get something out of you, even if it's nowhere near the initial asking price. I mean, seriously. How many people are going to have five million dollars to hand over? They can't really be expecting to get that; not unless they kidnap someone who they know is filthy rich. The fact that your brother doesn't have any money and you don't have any money, they realistically can't expect you to be handing over a huge amount."

John shrugged, unconvinced. "Hard to say. People like the kind we're dealing with here aren't always the most logical of thinkers."

"Many Filipinos think all foreigners are rich," Joy announced. "It's a very common way to think here."

"That's right," John agreed, "and you can't explain it to them that we're not. They just don't believe it if you tell them how it really is, that we're not all multimillionaires and that most people are barely getting by."

"That could make things harder with the ransom money then," Dan said and rubbed at his chin. "They probably won't believe you can't afford more, if that's the general mentality." Joy's revelation confused him. "Why do they think all foreigners are wealthy? It's hardly the case."

"What they see on American TV shows, I think," Joy said. "And a lot of foreigners with money visit the Philippines."

Dan nodded, then said, "If I'm going to do some digging on this, I'll need to team up with a local. Someone who speaks the language, someone locals are more likely to trust. I know many people speak some English here, but I'm sure most Filipinos are more comfortable speaking Tagalog."

"We mainly speak Bisaya in Cebu," Joy told him.

"That too," said Dan. "Either way, they'll trust a local more than me, and I'll need someone who knows their way around. I wouldn't have a clue."

Both John and Joy looked at each other, as if silently communicating. Joy broke eye contact with her husband and focused her gaze on Dan.

"I have a friend," she said. "She used to be in the PNP."

Dan said, "What's the PNP?"

"Philippine National Police. She knows people and has contacts. She's dealt with terrorists and Muslim extremists. She knows the area very well."

"She sounds perfect," Dan said.

"She's also very gwapa," Joy added.

When Dan looked confused, John explained, "Gwapa means beautiful."

CHAPTER THREE

Dan was up early the next day. He took a quick shower and made a coffee using the condiments supplied in the room. He tasted the brew. Not the best he'd ever had, but it would give him a kick start to the day at least. Breakfast was part of his deal while staying at the hotel, so he planned to venture downstairs shortly.

While he slowly drank his coffee he pondered his conversation with John and Joy the previous evening. He wasn't even really sure where to start in his search for Tyler Harvard. Maybe Joy's friend would have a better idea of where to begin.

Thinking about that drew his attention to the comment Joy had made about the woman being very beautiful. He really didn't see the relevance to the situation. After all, he was hardly here for a romantic rendezvous, so the woman's looks really weren't important.

Then again, he didn't really know the culture, so mentioning that she was "gwapa" might just be the Filipino thing to do.

His cell phone rang. When he checked the screen he saw that it was John.

"Hey John."

"Hi Dan. Just an update on your help. Her name is Carmen Mendoza and she'll meet you in your hotel lobby in an hour. Does that suit you?"

"Sure. That's fine. Any more calls from the kidnappers? Any

new developments?"

He heard John suck in a deep breath. "No, nothing yet."

"Okay. Keep me posted. I'll touch base with you later on today."

Dan had another coffee before going downstairs and dining on an American style breakfast, washed down with orange juice and more coffee. After that, he took a seat in the hotel lobby to await the arrival of Carmen Mendoza.

About ten minutes later he spied a woman enter through the hotel's huge front doors. She stood there gazing about, as if searching for someone. Dan figured that must be Carmen, so he waved from his seat until she spotted him and came on over.

The woman was maybe early thirties, but it was difficult to tell with Filipinas. She looked to be about five, five with a slender frame. Her hair was long and black and glistened under the artificial lights. Dressed in tight designer jeans and a fitted white top, Carmen had curves in all the right places. She was wearing sunglasses, but as Dan stood to greet her she removed them, and Dan saw exactly why Joy had called her gwapa.

She was stunningly beautiful like a Miss Universe entrant or top of the line catalog model. She smiled and shook his hand, hers soft in his.

For a brief moment he had to remind himself this was strictly business, and he couldn't allow anything to get in the way of that.

They introduced themselves, then sat down.

"Coffee?" Dan asked her. When she nodded, Dan signalled to a waiter who worked the small cafe in the lobby. He ordered two lattes, then returned his attention to Carmen. "Joy and John have filled you in about John's missing brother?"

"Yes, and it doesn't sound good," she said ominously.

"Why do you say that exactly? You don't think there's a chance they'll release Tyler?"

"We don't know who has him. That's what makes this even scarier," Carmen said honestly. "I don't think it's Abu Sayyaf or one of the known extremist groups. They're usually very quick to tell the world it's them who kidnapped a hostage. The fact that John received a phone call from the alleged kidnappers and they decided to remain anonymous tells me it's someone different. Someone we don't yet know about."

Dan pondered that. What Carmen said made sense, and she would know.

Carmen went on. "If it was Abu Sayyaf that would be frightening enough, but at least we'd know who we're dealing with. As of this moment we're completely in the dark and have no clue, so that will make negotiations harder and a possible rescue mission far more difficult."

"Maybe that's why they don't want us to know," Dan said. "Plus the fact that they won't want to end up in prison if they get caught." Their coffees arrived. Dan didn't bother adding sugar, just drank straight from the cup. "You'd know far more about this than me, but from my understanding, groups like Abu Sayyaf don't mind proclaiming that they're the guilty party because they feel untouchable. But if this is just a bunch of regular guys who one day decided to do a kidnap for ransom just to get some easy cash, then it's a totally different scenario for them if they get found out."

Carmen spooned three sugars into her latte. Dan had heard Filipinos generally had a sweet tooth.

"That's right," she agreed. "It's why I don't think it's one of the known groups of usual suspects. These people are likely what I would call freelancers, or opportunists. They may have a motive other than money, or it could just be a cash grab." She took a sip from her cup, coating her red lipstick with a light layer of froth.

"Do you think it could be someone Tyler knows?" Dan asked her. "You said they may have a motive other than money. Or as well as money."

"It's a possibility we need to look into."

"John said Tyler has no enemies."

Carmen shrugged. "John wouldn't know everything about his brother. There could be someone Tyler has never mentioned."

"True."

"The best person to talk to right now would be Tyler's wife," Carmen said, sounding like she'd made a decision.

Dan made a call to John and got the address of the relatives in Cebu where Larissa was staying. They finished their coffees, paid the bill, then left the hotel lobby and climbed into Carmen's car; a ruby red Toyota Rush.

As they drove to Larissa's location, the pair made small talk.

"Do you have a wife back in America, Dan?" Carmen asked casually.

"No, not anymore. I've been married twice and divorced twice," he was honest. "I figure maybe I'm just not that good at the whole relationship thing."

"What about girlfriends? Do you have one of those?"

"I have nobody in my life," he said, then realized the way he'd said it sounded a little melodramatic. He turned the same question on her. "I see no ring on your finger, so no husband then?"

"I was married when I was younger, but that was annulled." She glanced at Dan and blessed him with her smile. "We don't have divorces here. The Catholic Church doesn't believe in divorce."

"They have a lot of clout here then, a lot of power?"

"Yes. Too much in my opinion." Her smile flashed again. "I don't have a boyfriend either," she made a point of telling him. "Just in case you were wondering."

Noted, Dan thought, but it was time to change the subject before he got too distracted from the task at hand.

They entered an area outside of Cebu city called Mandaue as Dan idly chatted to her about his days on the force and asked her what it was like working for the police in the Philippines. It sounded similar, but yet also completely different to how it was in America.

"We're almost there," Carmen told him.

"I'm so glad you're with me," Dan said. "Otherwise I wouldn't have a clue where to go."

They passed a security guard on the way into a subdivision, which was basically a conglomeration of small houses and townhouses painted in yellow and pink. If they were new it would have looked like a candy store, but the entire place looked quite old and rundown. Even the concrete streets within were cracking up and crumbling.

Dogs and cats seemed to be running around everywhere, and an orange tricycle - a common form of short distance transportation - came roaring around a corner and very nearly collided with Carmen's Toyota. She hit the brakes and swerved to avoid the tricycle, narrowly avoiding having the paint scraped off the left side of her vehicle.

She shook her pretty head, but said nothing, just continued on, searching for the house address John had given them. Carmen brought the car to a stop outside a stand alone, single story house that was bordered by a chicken wire fence. A small black dog barked furiously at their arrival and looked anything but pleased to see them.

Dan was first out of the car, and stepping out of its air conditioning into the rising heat and humidity was a bit of a shock. He walked over and waited by the gate until Carmen joined him. They hadn't phoned ahead, so no one was expecting them. Would Larissa even be there?

A middle aged woman and a boy poked their heads out the open front door. The woman spoke something in the local dialect and Carmen answered. The only part Dan understood was the mention of Larissa's name.

Carmen opened the gate and stepped through. Dan followed. The angry black dog was tethered to the fence by a chain, so its gnashing teeth couldn't reach his ankles. The woman barked something at the dog, but it made zero difference to its demeanor.

Inside they found themselves in a living area that was cramped with too much seating. Dan and Carmen sat beside each other on a two seater sofa, while the woman disappeared down a hallway and knocked on a door. The young boy stood leaning against the wall staring at Dan like he'd never seen another human being before.

The middle aged woman returned and went into an adjoining kitchen. A moment later a young woman came down the hall, her long dark hair a little messed up like she'd been sleeping. Larissa eyed Dan and Carmen curiously, obviously wondering who they were and what they wanted.

Dan got to his feet. "I'm a good friend of John, Tyler's brother, and this is Carmen. We're here to help find your husband."

Larissa sat on the edge of an armchair and seemed to study them a moment. The boy still stared at Dan mostly.

"What can you tell us about the disappearance of your husband?" Carmen asked in a neutral tone.

Larissa chose to answer in Bisaya. Dan could do nothing but watch Carmen nod from time to time. When Larissa seemed to be finished, he asked a question of his own.

"Does Tyler have any enemies? Is there any reason someone might want to do him harm?"

The woman didn't speak, just shook her head.

Dan leaned forward on the couch. "And what about you, Larissa? Is there anyone you can think of who might have kidnapped Tyler to get at you?"

For a moment Larissa seemed a little shocked when she realized he was asking if she had any enemies, but she shook her head again.

"I don't know anyone," she said in a soft voice.

"Is that your mother in the kitchen?" Carmen asked, and Larissa nodded. "Is there anything she might be able to tell us that will help?"

Again the young woman shook her head, then her entire body started to tremble as tears welled in her eyes. Just as Larissa started to cry, her mother returned to the living room carrying a tray loaded up with glasses of water and a plate of local snacks that looked like tiny, crunchy pieces of bread. The older woman placed the tray on a coffee table and then hugged her daughter, caressing her head like she were a child.

Both Dan and Carmen gave them a minute. Dan took the opportunity to take a sip of water, but he didn't try the snacks.

"She very upset," the mother spoke in English. "Scared for her husband."

Carmen now picked up some water and took a few mouthfuls before replacing the glass on the table.

"Larissa?" she said calmly. "Are you sure there's no one who would want to do you or Tyler harm?"

With tears still streaming down Larissa's face, she said rather sharply, "I can't think of anybody. Just find my husband. Please." The final word was drawn out in a heartfelt plea.

Dan sucked in a deep breath and looked at Carmen. She nodded toward the door, indicating they might as well go, so they excused themselves and left.

Talking to Tyler's wife had proved to be a total dead end.

CHAPTER FOUR

Tyler was still in the same room. It'd been four days and he hadn't left it once. The only addition from the first night was a bucket for him to use as a toilet and a blanket riddled with holes, like someone had opened up on it with a machine gun while it was hanging on the line.

The bucket was emptied once a day by a teenage boy whose name was Joven. That same boy also brought him food and water once a day, usually as the sun was going down. He was always accompanied by an armed guard.

Right now the mid-morning sun was streaming in through the barred window, increasing the heat to unbearable levels. He knew the heat would only get worse. Sweat was dripping down his skin in rivers and his clothes, the same clothes he'd been wearing since he was nabbed, felt totally disgusting. His shirt was gluing to his back like it had been wallpapered on and he smelled worse than a skunk.

He knew now that he'd been kidnapped for ransom, but he had no clue by who, nor where he was currently located. One of the guys who'd taken him from the restaurant the other night had been in to see him the day before and told Tyler that they were going to make a ransom demand to his brother, John. Somehow they already seemed to know Tyler had an older brother, but didn't tell him how. And whenever Tyler asked a question of his own, he was met with nothing but stony silence.

The man had said they'd be asking John for five million US dollars, an incredible amount that Tyler knew had no chance of being paid. John didn't have a lot of money and neither did Tyler.

Ever since then he'd been worried about what was going to happen to him. There was no way five million was going to be paid. He knew John would do his best to offer up something, but would his abductors accept an amount that was obviously going to be way less than what they were asking for?

Tyler sure hoped so, but he had his doubts.

He went to the window and gazed out at the jungle. There were a few wooden buildings visible through gaps in the trees. He had a feeling he was still on Cebu island, but somewhere out in the provinces. No breeze came through the bars, nothing to alleviate the increasing heat and humidity. He was also out of water and probably wouldn't get any more until this evening. The constant thirst was just another thing to add to his current misery.

His thoughts turned to Larissa, as they had numerous times since he'd been taken. He wondered how she was holding up. He worried about her, knowing that she'd be beside herself, scared to death about what had happened to him. He loved her like he'd never loved before and just prayed that he'd get out of this and make it back to her alive.

CHAPTER FIVE

Next on the agenda was visiting the NBI agent in charge of Tyler's kidnapping investigation. Carmen personally knew the man and had worked with him several times in the past. However, he overall opinion of him wasn't a particularly positive one.

"Diaryo Ramos can be lazy," she said as she drove them towards the NBI building in Central Cebu, which ended up being located not too far away from Dan's hotel.

Dan nodded as he gazed out the car window. "Is he corrupt or on the take do you think?" He looked at Carmen now.

"I don't think so," she said. "In that way I believe he's okay. I just think he has a pretty sweet position and doesn't like to extend too much effort. That's just my opinion based on experience working with him before."

"So, is there any point in going to see this guy then?" Dan asked pointedly. "I know he's in charge officially, but if he really couldn't care less, then what use is he to us?"

"He might know something that he hasn't shared yet," Carmen said. "Anyway, I think it's important that we keep him informed, just in case we do end up needing him."

We have nothing to inform him about so far, Dan thought, but didn't voice it.

Carmen found a parking space as close as she could to the

building that housed the Cebu branch of the National Bureau of Investigation and killed the motor. As they walked towards the building they passed a group of three woman loitering on the street eating snacks and chatting. The women paused mid conversation and all stared at Dan as he and Carmen strolled by.

"Lami Americano," one of them said and smiled mischievously.

Dan turned to Carmen. "What did that woman just say?"

Carmen grinned. "She was saying you are a tasty and yummy American."

"Yummy?" Dan bobbed his head from side to side. "Can't say anyone has ever called me yummy before."

"Some Filipinas are not that fussy when it comes to foreigners," she told him, still smiling.

"Thanks."

The pair entered the NBI building. Carmen immediately went over to a Reception desk and asked to speak with Agent Ramos if he was available. Turned out he was and they were ushered through to a waiting area with worn, but comfortable seating. Five minutes later and they were in his office, perched on chairs that were not as cozy as those in the waiting room.

Agent Diaryo Ramos was about fifty, stocky in build and completely bald. Dan had shaken his meaty hand before taking a seat and was surprised when the man's soft grip defied his powerful looking build.

Dan sat there while Ramos and Carmen conversed in their local language for a spell, but eventually Ramos looked at Dan and stated,

"I don't believe Mr. Harvard was kidnapped by Abu Sayyaf. I've spoken with my contacts in Mindanao and all the known militant groups deny any knowledge of the matter."

"So that means he was either kidnapped by pure chance," Dan mused, "or by someone closer to home."

"Meaning?" Ramos raised an eyebrow and gave Dan a look that might have said he had no business being involved in this.

"Meaning someone has a vested interest in his kidnapping," Dan explained. "It could be personal as well as financial."

Ramos looked at Carmen when he asked his next question. "And you have evidence of this?"

"No," she answered honestly. "It's just a suspicion based on the fact that his kidnappers are a mystery and don't want to identify themselves." Carmen sighed. "You know how it works here, Diaryo. If a foreigner is kidnapped, someone puts their hand up to take responsibility. Maybe Tyler Harvard was just a random target for some opportunists, or he was deliberately targeted, which makes it personal. If it's personal, then it's either someone he knows, or someone who knows *him* at least."

Ramos thought about this for a while, then slowly nodded his meaty head. "Okay. We'll dig deeper into the people Mr. Harvard knows and regularly associates with. See if we can uncover a motive and a lead to his whereabouts." He turned his gaze on Dan. "Has your friend had any more calls for ransom demands?"

"Not last time I checked," Dan said. "I'm sure he would have called me if he'd heard from them again."

"When he does hear from them," Ramos said. "And he will, be sure to let me know."

The tone of the agent's voice sounded like they'd been dismissed. Carmen thanked Ramos for his time as they stood up and left the office.

"That seemed like a waste of time as well," Dan noted once they were back out in the hot sun.

"I did say he is a bit on the lazy side. Doesn't like to do too much."

Dan sucked in a deep breath. "I have a feeling if we're going to get Tyler back alive, it's going to be up to us."

They decided to stop at Ayala Center for lunch, which was Cebu's largest shopping mall. The place was huge, with multiple stories, loads of stores, cinemas, and restaurants and cafes catering to everyone's tastes; local or foreign. It looked like a good spot to find some food he actually felt like eating.

On the second floor terrace Dan spotted a place called 'Army Navy'. It caught his attention, so he stopped to check out the menu. Big, meaty burgers, fries and shakes. Just the kind of junk food he was craving. When he looked at Carmen, she didn't look so certain. She had her sights on a place a few stores down that looked like it sold Filipino food. He handed her a one thousand peso note.

"You get what you want there, I'll get something in here, and we'll meet up at one of these outside tables," he said.

She nodded and off she went.

Dan didn't have to wait long inside the store, and soon he was seated at an outdoor table waiting for his food to arrive. Carmen appeared carrying a plate loaded up with rice and other assorted local food. She sat down opposite him, cracked open a bottle of water, took a sip and gazed about.

A waiter brought Dan's food to the table and he quickly tucked into some fries and cheese sauce, washing them down with sips of an icy cold chocolate shake.

"I'm not sure there's much we can do right now," Dan said after taking the first bite from his burger. It tasted pretty awesome. "We have no leads to follow. I'm thinking we might have to wait until the kidnappers call John again with further instructions. At least then we'll have some sort of lead to follow."

Carmen spooned some food into her mouth and chewed away on it while also chewing over what Dan had just said. Eventually she nodded and drank some more water.

"I want to be there when they call again," she said. "It'll be better if I negotiate the deal anyway."

Dan said, "I agree. Chances are they'll call back at night like last time, so I'll text John and tell him we'll be over later."

He sent John a text, then finished his food in silence and realized Carmen was only halfway done. Was he eating like a pig, or was she just a slow eater?

"So you've retired from the PNP. What do you do now?" he asked. "That is, when you're not running around playing private detective with me."

"I have some businesses that are doing okay," Carmen answered.

"I also have reliable and honest staff, so I don't usually need to be there myself."

"What type of businesses?"

"One is a water station."

"What's that? Distilled drinking water?"

She nodded. "I also have a Sari Sari store, which is like a small convenience store. Lechon manok." When Dan looked at her blankly, she added, "Roast chicken shop. And I also run a small bar which is only open at nights."

"Wow. Sounds like you should be really busy."

"I would be if I didn't set everything up in such a way that I don't have to run it all. That's why having just the right staff is so important. It can be really hard to find reliable and honest workers, so I've been really lucky."

"And smart," Dan noted.

Carmen smiled coyly. "Maybe a little bit of that too." She stood up. "Talking about business, I should do the rounds and see how things are going."

Dan's phone chimed and he checked his messages. "John and Joy are going to make us dinner," he told her as he stood.

"Okay. I'll drop you back at your hotel and pick you up again at six."

*****

After a short nap in the comfort of the hotel air conditioning, Dan spent the remainder of the afternoon doing some research on his laptop. He studied up on hostage negotiations, particularly in the

Philippines, some kidnap for ransom cases orchestrated by the infamous Abu Sayyaf, and the NBI and PNP in general. By the time he was done he was certainly no expert, but at least now had a bit more background on how everything worked in this country.

Carmen arrived right on time and once more Dan found himself being chauffeured around Cebu city by the exotically beautiful woman.

Traffic was a little on the heavy side and they didn't get to John's place until after six thirty.

The dinner table boasted mainly a selection of local dishes again, but there was a large plate of fried chicken that Dan was happy about.

Everyone sat at the table after a short prayer of thanksgiving from Joy.

"Today drew a blank," Dan said. "We had a chat to Larissa, then Agent Ramos, but neither proved very helpful. Ramos says he will dig deeper, but I wouldn't count on it."

John looked very worried, and was probably feeling as useless as Dan was right now. Joy patted her husband's hand reassuringly. Their two kids were oblivious to the drama going on and were happily digging into the food already.

"Let's hope the scum holding Tyler call tonight," John said bitterly. "Then we might be able to make some progress at least."

John seemed disinterested in eating, and Dan didn't really feel all that hungry himself, but he forced himself to eat a little. Carmen and Joy piled up their plates with food, and eventually John succumbed and gathered up some rice, vegetables and fried chicken.

"Is there any way we can trace the call if and when it comes in?" Dan wondered. He now wished he had Jenkins here with him, his tech guy.

John said, "The number was blocked, and if it's a cell phone, I'm not sure how."

"Hard to triangulate too," Carmen chimed in, "without having the number or a general idea of the location. Impossible to track by GPS too without first installing an app on the target phone."

After dinner was done, everything had been cleaned up and the kids were in their room entertaining themselves, John brought some beers and a bottle of wine into the living room. As soon as Carmen saw the alcohol she shook her head adamantly.

"I don't think that's a good idea just now," she said. "We all need clear heads if these people do call with instructions."

John looked like he was about to argue the point, but then seemed to realize she was right. He slumped into the lounge with a heavy sigh.

"A part of me really feels like numbing myself with alcohol," he said to no one in particular, but then he looked at Carmen. "You're right, though. We all need to have clear heads right now, for Tyler's sake."

"If they call," Carmen said, "put your phone on speaker phone so we can all hear, and so I can communicate with them. I think it's best if I do the negotiating, but you talk to them first, John. If I answer right away it might freak them out."

As they sat around waiting with anticipation, thunder rumbled in the distance, signaling an oncoming storm. It still sounded quite distant, but in the tropics the weather could change very rapidly.

John checked his phone for the umpteenth time and made sure it wasn't somehow on silent mode.

"Don't worry, mate," Dan said. "You'll hear it if it rings."

"I really need to go pee," John said.

"Be quick."

And he was, back next to his wife on the lounge in less than a minute.

"I still feel like a beer," he said and kept fidgeting on the lounge. Joy put her head on his shoulder in a bid to keep him calm. John's arm slipped around his wife and he held her close.

Time dragged on. Dan kept looking at his watch almost as often as John had been checking his phone. Thunder reverberated across the sky, closer now, and just as the first fat drops of rain spattered down on the metal roof, John's cell phone rang.

He eyed the phone like it was possessed at first, then answered it and put it on speaker.

"Hello?"

"John Harvard?" came a voice with a distinctive local accent.

"Speaking," John said and fidgeted nervously on the couch again.

"Here are the instructions for ransom payment of five million dollars."

"Ah...wait-" John began, until Carmen cut him off and spoke in rapid Bisaya to the guy on the other end of the line. She then suddenly switched to English.

"I will deliver the ransom money and negotiate the release of the hostage," Carmen said firmly. "But the amount won't be five million US dollars."

Silence on the other end.

When she received no reply, Carmen put forth John's offer. "The amount will be fifty thousand US dollars, in cash." She paused, then added. "That's all we have."

"I'll call you back," the kidnapper said and immediately disconnected the call.

"Now I feel really nervous," said John. "It's weird. I've been in combat situations before and never felt nervous like I am right now."

"It's because it's your brother and you feel like you have no control over the situation," Dan surmised, then realized his statement probably wasn't too helpful.

John said, "I hope he calls back, and that they agree to that amount."

"He'll call back," Carmen was confident. "Fifty thousand dollars is like winning the lotto for many Filipinos. I doubt they'll say no to it."

"You're probably right," John said, trying to sound confident.

"Just try and relax. We'll get this resolved soon and get Tyler back."

Dan sat there trying to be optimistic himself. There were still so many unknowns, but at least the men had made contact, a deal had been put to them, and hopefully they'd take it and this mess would soon be cleared up.

The rain was coming down steadily now. The metal roof amplified every single drop. If it got any heavier and the kidnappers called back, they'd barely be able to hear the conversation.

Lightning illuminated the scene outside, followed almost instantly by a tremendous crack of thunder. For a moment Dan felt like he was back in the jungles of Purgatory Island, in the midst of that horrendous hurricane he and his friends had endured. That had been hell on earth. This was no hurricane though, just a thunderstorm, and he was safe and sound inside John's house.

Another twenty minutes passed before John's phone finally rang again. Thankfully the rain wasn't too heavy and they could all hear the kidnapper's voice when John put it on speaker phone.

"We accept your deal," the man spoke slowly and emotionless. "Now listen carefully."

CHAPTER SIX

The rain had been pelting down for well over an hour now, and the thunder and lightning were unlike anything Tyler had witnessed before. It was as if the sky was alive with electricity and intense anger. The weather was a nice reprieve from the heat and humidity, and he found himself wishing he could stand out there in the rain and wash the sweat and grime from his clammy skin.

As he watched out the window a bolt shot down from the heavens and exploded somewhere in the jungle not too far away. He really hoped no one was nearby, or they'd be cooked for sure.

Still, he'd rather be taking his chances out there in the storm than be locked away in this cell, not knowing what was going to happen next.

Tyler didn't know if he was going to get out of this alive. Living in the Philippines for a number of years, he'd heard about all the kidnap for ransom stories on the news. Some hostages were released if a ransom was paid, while others barbarically had their heads severed off with a large knife.

He shuddered at the thought and couldn't help but think about what those final moments would feel like. So far he hadn't been made to make any videos pleading for his release and for the ransom to be paid, but he'd seen those on the internet. The strange thing was, many of the victims appeared calm, like they were resigned to their fate.

They must have been terrified on the inside though.

His cigarettes had run out days ago and his kidnappers hadn't given him any more, even though he'd asked for some. Right now he felt like he'd do anything for a few puffs on a smoke to calm his nerves.

Images of Larissa's sweet, pretty face entered his mind and it made him smile a sad smile. She was the best thing that had ever happened to him, having come to the Philippines to find a wife at his brother's urging. It was the smartest decision he'd ever made and he hadn't been happier.

Now everything was uncertain. Maybe that blissful existence was over and he'd never see her again? She was innocent in all of this and so was he. They didn't deserve what was happening and he still couldn't quite believe it all.

He pinched himself, but it wasn't a dream. It was a living nightmare.

Tyler was suddenly startled out of his reverie by a sound outside. The cell door flew open and smashed against the concrete wall. Then two men entered, pointing automatic weapons in his direction.

CHAPTER SEVEN

The deal was going down tomorrow night. After instructions had been given, John had cracked open that beer and drank it quickly. Dan had joined him in a brew while Carmen and Joy had nursed a glass of wine each.

While they had a drink to settle their nerves, Carmen had tried to get in touch with Agent Ramos, but couldn't reach him.

An hour later she'd suggested she and Dan leave. With nothing really to do until the next evening, Carmen had driven them to her bar so they could have a few quiet drinks together.

"It won't be busy tonight," she said as she parked the car. "Especially not in weather like this."

Her bar was located in a side street just off from one of the main roads. With the rain still coming down quite heavily, no one was on the streets except for a couple of stray dogs desperately in search of a meal.

When Dan looked up at a sign painted with the bar's name, he laughed.

Stray Cats

Carmen grinned. "That's because there were loads of stray cats hanging around here when I first opened up," she explained.

Dan pointed out the dogs rummaging around in the wet. "You might have to change the name to *Stray Dogs* tonight."

They exited the car and dashed through the rain to reach the cover of the bar. Once inside, Dan noted there were only three guys sitting at one of the tables drinking a local beer called Red Horse. Behind the well stocked bar was a attractive young woman of maybe about twenty. A young man was walking around sweeping the floor, intermittently wiping the tables over with a damp cloth. Lounge music set to a low volume emanated from speakers placed around the bar.

Carmen greeted her staff, then led Dan to a table by the front windows. While the bar was quite small and cozy, they were far enough away from the three guys drinking beer that they could talk in confidence.

The young woman came out from behind the bar and made her way over to her boss.

"What would you like to drink?" Carmen asked him.

"Do you have Jim Beam bourbon?"

"I think we have some of that left. It's only popular with foreigners, but we get a few in here."

"I like it with Coke and ice, thanks."

The young barmaid nodded.

"Just get me a San Miguel Light," Carmen said and the woman moved off to fetch their drinks. In no time the girl was back. "Salamat."

"That means 'thank you'," Dan said and smiled. "I know one word."

"It's a start."

Dan tried his drink. It tasted good. Sometimes when he drank alcohol he still wished he smoked cigarettes, as the two went so well together. He pushed that urge aside though. There was no way he was taking up that habit again.

"You said you were married twice," Carmen said after sampling her beer. "Did you have any children?"

Dan shook his head. "No. No kids. How about you?"

"It's quite common for Filipinos to start having families quite young, but I was too focused on my career for that."

"So that's a no then?"

Carmen nodded. She put her elbow on the table and rested her head in the palm of her hand. Her dark eyes were sparkling as she looked at Dan. Or maybe it was just the effects of alcohol?

"Those women were right earlier today," she said softly.

"What women?"

"The ones outside the NBI building. The woman said you were a yummy American."

Dan felt himself blush, not expecting the sudden compliment from her. The look in Carmen's eyes was also making him a little nervous, but in a good way, an exciting way.

"Salamat," he said, then felt rather stupid. He cleared his throat and took a sip of his bourbon. "Can I be totally honest?"

"Sure." She smiled, head still resting on her palm, her eyes never leaving Dan's.

"You are one of the most beautiful women I've ever seen."

Carmen tilted her head back and laughed. "Thank you," she said.

Dan said, "Now I feel awkward."

"Don't." Carmen took a long pull on her beer while Dan downed some more bourbon. "How far away is your hotel from here?" she asked. "Not too far, is it?" Dan shrugged. "How about we have one more drink here, then go back there and raid the mini bar."

One hour and several more drinks later they were naked in Dan's hotel bed going for gold. Their lovemaking was fast, furious and urgent, both desperately needing to release pent up sexual tension.

When they'd been satisfied, Dan lay back against the pillows. He was sweating despite having the air conditioner set to the coldest level.

"I think...we both...needed that," Carmen stammered, a little out of breath.

"Yes, and I think we both need another drink to put out the flames," Dan quipped and got out of bed to remove two beers from the bar fridge. He ripped the caps off, handed one to Carmen, then flopped back onto the bed.

In a way he felt a little guilty indulging in personal pleasure while Tyler was still missing, but there really wasn't anything they could do about it right now anyway. Not until tomorrow night, when they'd put a plan into action.

"Cheers," Dan said and tapped his beer bottle against hers.

Carmen had her breathing under control now and looked quite relaxed.

"You're my first foreigner," she admitted. "And I certainly wasn't disappointed." She took a sip. "If we do it again, we should go for some slow, intimate and much longer lovemaking."

Dan smiled. "I agree, but we both needed it hard and fast just now."

"We sure did."

Carmen leaned over and kissed him tenderly on the cheek. It felt so nice to be close to a woman again like this, Dan thought. It'd been a while. He really enjoyed her company and there was definitely a lot of chemistry between them. He just wished they'd met under more positive circumstances, where they could freely enjoy their time together.

Carmen asked, "Is it okay if I spend the night?"

He nodded. "I'd love that. You'll even get a free hotel breakfast in the morning."

"Really?"

He nodded again. "This room is for two people anyway, so two breakfasts are included in the price."

Carmen sipped her beer and grinned. "A long night of making love followed by a free breakfast. It doesn't get any better than that."

Now Dan smiled. "I don't disappoint on a first date."

"No, you certainly don't."

CHAPTER EIGHT

The kidnappers didn't want the equivalent of fifty thousand US dollars in Philippine currency. They wanted actual US dollars. John had seen his bank the next morning and arranged the withdrawal of the exact amount, which he placed into a bag. Dan had accompanied him to the bank while Carmen remained with Joy at their place.

Dan had silently chastised himself as they left the bank. He was feeling tired and lethargic after a night of making love to Carmen multiple times, a little too much alcohol and definitely not enough sleep. While the experience had been fantastic, he hadn't wanted to jeopardize Tyler's safety because his hormones were working overtime.

They had finally managed to get in touch with Agent Diaryo Ramos and told him about the ransom drop off and exchange for Tyler's freedom. The man had assured them he'd have a team on hand, that he would personally lead, to guarantee everything went smoothly and that the offenders would be apprehended.

Dan didn't plan to wait for Ramos and go with him. He and Carmen would make their own way to the exchange point. The kidnappers had said they were to come alone anyway, so it was better if they didn't all show up together and spook them.

As the sun started to set over the hills behind Cebu, Dan, John, Carmen and Joy all gathered at John's house to make last minute preparations for tonight's mission.

Joy disappeared into the kitchen to make some food for everyone. The kids were in their room doing homework.

Carmen, through her contacts, had managed to get her hands on a small GPS tracking device, which Dan now hid in the lining of the bag that contained the ransom money. Dan wanted it as insurance, in case they got separated from the money before they had Tyler. Carmen had also scored Dan a handgun, even though he wasn't legally allowed to carry one in the Philippines. Being legal was the least of his concerns right now though.

"I really should be going too," John protested. "He is *my* brother."

Dan held up his hand. "We've been through this. It's too dangerous for you. You have a wife and kids to look after. You also don't want to do anything that might jeopardize your residency here. Besides, if things don't go to plan we'll need you on the outside as backup. Carmen and I can handle it, and Ramos and his team will be there as well."

John nodded reluctantly, but still looked unconvinced. Dan totally understood John's position and where he was coming from, but it was best he take a back seat on this. He'd already done his part in a huge way by getting the money together. There was no point in putting himself in the firing line.

An hour later and they had dinner. The rendezvous time was still some hours away. Dan felt nervous with anticipation. He was itching to get this done, but was forced to wait.

"Don't take Carmen's car," John suggested. "It's too flashy. They might decide they want that as well and leave you all stranded. Take my old pickup. No one would give that beast a second look."

"Okay," Dan agreed. It made sense. The less conspicuous they were overall, the better. They didn't want to look like they had more money than they were willing to offer, as it could send the deal south.

To help keep himself alert, Dan had several strong coffees while they were waiting. He'd felt tired and lethargic earlier, but now, with the caffeine in his system and the adrenalin starting to course through his veins, he felt wide awake and ready for action.

When it was time to go, Dan took the keys to John's old faded blue pickup and got behind the wheel. Carrying the bag of cash, Carmen sat in the passenger seat.

"We'll keep in contact," Dan said to John. "And don't worry. We'll get Tyler back."

Following Carmen's directions, Dan drove west through the city until they were driving up into the mountains that divided the island and pretty much left civilization behind them.

The evening was clear, the stars bright in a black sky. They were headed towards a township called Bonbon, with the exchange to take place in a location just on the outskirts of town. According to Carmen, most of that area was forest and jungle; the perfect hideout for kidnappers.

Every now and then Dan spied a structure near the side of the road, or lights flickering amidst the foliage, but for the most part the region was devoid of people. The road continued to wind its way through the hilltops, and there was no traffic around at that hour to impede their progress. Eventually, when they passed through an area called Babag, Carmen lightly touched his arm.

"We'll be turning off onto another road shortly, on the left," she said.

Dan found the turnoff and followed a narrower, bumpier road for a few minutes before suddenly there was a little township.

"Is this Bonbon?" he asked.

"No. Keep going. It's not far now though."

Carmen was studying a Google map on her smartphone so she could pinpoint the exact location of the drop off zone. They were to meet at a particular basketball court near Bonbon, and that's where the exchange would take place.

Dan checked his watch and saw it was a little after ten. The rendezvous time was eleven PM. He'd wanted to get there early and it looked like that would be the case.

As they entered the Bonbon area there were clusters of houses and stores here and there, then stretches where there wasn't much of anything.

"Turn left here," Carmen told him and Dan swung the old twin cab pickup onto a rutted dirt road that snaked its way through a jungle zone.

"There's a basketball court down he?" he asked her, feeling doubtful.

"According to the map, yes."

Dan kept going, driving slowly now. Soon the jungle opened up a little and a dark domed structure materialized out of the gloom. The only hint of light came from one small lit bulb on the far corner of the basketball court. He didn't see any other vehicles about, nor were there any houses nearby that he could make out.

It was a strange location for a community basketball court, set amidst the jungle and not really near anyone who lived in the area. Not exactly convenient.

Dan drove the car under a grove of trees and killed the engine, but left the parking lights on for the moment to provide a little bit of light without putting a huge drain on the battery. From the glove box he retrieved a small flashlight and got out. He looked about a little nervously. The entire place was surrounded by thick foliage. Anyone could creep up on them from any direction. He took the gun out from his waistband and hefted the weight of it in his hand.

Would he need it, and would one handgun be enough?

Replacing the gun behind his back, Dan wandered slowly around the clearing, then made his way over to the basketball court. The interior was completely dark, and the access gates had chains and padlocks on them. That single bulb did little to illuminate the area, and the pickup's parking lights didn't reach that far.

He flicked on the flashlight and played it over the interior of the court, then aimed the beam towards the jungle on his right and swept its edges. Glancing back towards the car, he saw Carmen standing beside it with the passenger door ajar. She was looking around nervously as well.

Dan walked back to the car, all the while still searching the jungle with his flashlight.

"Any word from Ramos?" he asked in a soft voice as he came up to her side. Carmen shook her head. "When he does get here, I hope he's smart enough to be discreet about it."

Dan texted John to tell him they'd arrived at the location, but nothing was happening yet. John very quickly replied with a simple 'OK'.

Up in the hilltops it was still warm and muggy, but maybe a little better than down in the city. Dan was lightly sweating, but he wasn't sure if that was from the climate or nervous anticipation. Maybe both.

He checked his watch and saw that it was ten minutes to eleven. Getting close now. His heart rate increased a few beats.

Where the hell was Ramos? Was he on his way? Were his men already in position, hiding in the darkness somewhere nearby?

He turned to Carmen and whispered. "Give Ramos a call and find out where he is. It's nearly time."

Carmen took her phone from her pocket, pressed a few buttons and put it to her ear. Thirty seconds later she hung up. "He's not answering his phone."

"Shit," Dan hissed in a low voice. "Let's just hope he shows up. We might need him." He really didn't want to have to rely on the guy though. With any luck this would all go smoothly and they'd be out of there soon, with Tyler.

Dan's watch ticked past eleven PM and there was still no sign of action. He felt like pacing around, but was reluctant to leave the car or Carmen. And there was that big bag of money inside too.

Nothing happened for a further five minutes, then a lone figure emerged out of the darkness from the jungle at the opposite end of the basketball court. It was a Filipino man, walking slowly and looked to be unarmed, as far as Dan could tell from a distance in the gloom. He tried to spy movement behind the man or anywhere else, but nothing stirred, just this guy seemingly all on his own.

"I don't see Tyler," Carmen whispered, stating the obvious.

Dan reached a hand behind his back and rested his fingers on the handle of the gun, preparing to pull it out and use it if he had to.

The man continued to approach with a slow gait. When he was about twenty feet away from them, he said, "Where is the money?"

"Where's Tyler?" Dan growled back, not happy at all about the guy asking for the cash when Tyler clearly wasn't with him. Dan looked the man over. He was quite skinny and didn't hold a weapon. That didn't mean he didn't have one on him somewhere. "Where is Tyler, your hostage?" Dan said again when he got no response.

"You get him when you hand over the money."

"No way." It was Carmen who spoke now. "This is an exchange process. The money for Tyler, done at the same time. That's not negotiable."

The guy looked a little confused, so Carmen repeated her words in Bisaya. The man shook his head and returned his attention to Dan.

"First you give me the money," he said. "Then we bring your friend."

"Where is he?" Dan asked again. "Is he nearby? Are you here all alone?"

"He not here."

Dan's hand was still behind his back. "I've had enough of this shit." He withdrew the pistol and pointed it at the Filipino's head. "Bring me Tyler right now or I'm gonna put a hole where your brain's supposed to be."

The man remained calm and impassive. He certainly didn't look afraid. The guy glanced at Carmen and spoke in rapid Bisaya.

"He just told me that if you don't drop the gun you'll be shot," Carmen informed Dan.

Dan shrugged. "Shot by who?"

"One of us," a voice said from behind them.

Both Dan and Carmen swung around simultaneously and found themselves staring down the barrels of rifles held by two men. Dan spotted a few more armed men coming out of the jungle behind the first wave.

He had no choice but to ditch his pistol in the dirt.

CHAPTER NINE

Carmen and Dan were walked through the jungle at gun point for about a mile and a half. The first man who'd appeared at the rendezvous was carrying the bag of money. Dan was walking right behind him, feeling pissed off that these guys had John's cash, and them, and there was still no sign of Tyler.

Where the fuck was Ramos? He and his men obviously weren't anywhere nearby or they would have done something, surely.

They arrived in an area where the jungle was more sparse. Lights shone in several wooden buildings almost hidden amid some trees over to the left. On the right was a small concrete hut that was topped with a metal roof. The men guided Dan and Carmen in the direction of the hut, a door was unlocked and they were ushered inside.

Before the door was slammed shut, one of the armed men said, "Maybe next time you won't pull a gun on us. All you had to do was hand over the money."

Dan turned to the man who'd spoken and said, "And why would I have done that? The cash was supposed to be a swap for Tyler, the man you kidnapped off the street. Where the hell is he?"

The only answer he got to his question was the butt of a rifle in his abdomen. Dan grunted as he doubled up in pain. He went down on his knees just as the door to the hut was slammed shut and locked, leaving him alone in there with Carmen.

"Dan," she said, getting down beside him and placing a reassuring hand on his back. "Are you okay?"

He nodded, looking at the floor. "I will be...in a minute."

When he'd recovered enough from the blow to stand, he got back to his feet. They may have taken his gun and their cell phones, but the flashlight was still in his pocket and he used it to look around the small room. There was absolutely nothing in there except four walls, a roof and the concrete floor.

On the wall opposite the entrance door was a small window with rusted metal bars on it, effectively preventing any chance of escape that way. Dan moved over to the window and peered out, trying to see what he could make out in the darkness. He shone the light outside, but it didn't reach very far. Mostly all he could see out there was jungle.

Turning away from the window he moved the torch beam over the concrete floor. Something caught his eye and he squatted down to check it out. Dan picked up something brown, rectangular and flat. When he held it under the light he realized it was a cigarette butt that had been stamped out under a boot or shoe.

He sniffed it. Smelled like ash, so he tossed it back on the floor and stood up again.

"Tyler smokes," he said, mostly to himself. "I wonder if they had him in here. And if they did, why isn't he still here?"

"Now we're in the same situation as him," Carmen said, sounding stressed. "I was the negotiator, the one who was supposed to get him free. Now we're all hostages."

Dan wrapped his arms around her in an attempt to reassure her.

"We shouldn't have come up here with just the two of us. I should have arranged for some backup to be nearby."

"That was supposed to be what Agent Ramos and his team were," Carmen spat, clearly annoyed. "Why didn't he answer his phone, and why didn't he show up?"

Dan didn't have an answer to that. He didn't have answers to anything just now. All he did know was that they had to find a way to escape. Only then could they do anything more to help Tyler, and themselves.

A thought occurred to him then and it gave him a glimmer of hope.

"Maybe he got away," he barely whispered.

"Sorry? What did you say?"

"Tyler. Maybe he escaped. Maybe that's why they didn't bring him to the trade, because they no longer had him, but they still wanted to get their hands on the money."

"I hope you're right, Dan, and that he's somewhere safe." She looked up at him, her dark brown eyes having lost their usual confidence. "But what about us? What are *we* going to do?"

"We're going to figure a way out of here, that's what we're going to do."

He did his best to make it sound like he had a firm resolve, for her sake, but in reality he didn't have a clue what he was going to do to pull off the promise he'd just made to her.

His watch told him it was now well after midnight and all was dead quiet outside. Where were the kidnappers holed up? Did they live in those wooden houses nestled in the jungle?

He wished there was a window in the door as well, or the sides of their concrete prison cell. At least then he could get a much better overall view of the area and maybe determine where everyone was. Just the one vantage point didn't offer much information at all.

Dan went back to the window and shone the flashlight on the rusted bars. He seized one in his free hand and gave it a firm tug. Despite the age and rust, it felt very solid. He tried a second bar with the same conclusion. Without tools they weren't escaping out the window.

He went over to the door then. It opened inwards, so there was no chance of putting his boot to it and kicking it open. The hinges weren't accessible either, even if he had a knife or a screwdriver. Optimistically he tried the handle, but sure enough the door was locked. Still, he put the flashlight on the floor, gripped the handle with both hands, propped one foot against the wall for leverage and tried with all his might to pull the door open.

Wasn't gonna happen.

"What are you doing?" Carmen wanted to know.

"Trying to get us out of here."

"You look like you're going to injure yourself."

Dan felt deflated as he realized he was basically out of options. He focused the torch beam on the roof, but he couldn't see any possible avenue of escape there.

He wasn't prepared to give up though. There must be a way.

Maybe he just needed to chill out for a while and let some thoughts come to him. Stress made it harder to think rationally, so he figured he needed to calm his mind.

Dan sat on the floor below the window and leaned his back against the wall. Carmen joined him and rested her head on his shoulder.

He smiled ironically. "Tonight is a hell of a lot different to last night," he mused.

Now Carmen smiled in the darkness, also recalling the fun they'd had. "I wish we were back in your hotel room right now."

"Yeah. Anywhere would be better than this place."

He closed his eyes, intending to clear his head and see if any ideas came to him, but he felt really tired, so tired in fact that he dozed off after just a few minutes.

Dan's eyes suddenly snapped open. He wasn't sure what had woken him. Feeling groggy, he checked his watch and saw that it was edging towards three in the morning. He'd been asleep for hours. Carmen's head still rested on his shoulder as she continued to slumber.

Feeling a little stiff, he got to his feet, his movement waking Carmen up in the process.

"What's wrong?" she asked.

"Something woke me, but I'm not sure what."

He listened intently in the darkness. Suddenly there was a loud crack, the unmistakable sound of a gunshot. He went to the window and peered out. Couldn't see a thing out there. Now excited voices could be heard, along with the sound of footsteps thudding toward their prison hut. The lock disengaged and the door swung open.

One of the kidnappers pointed his rifle into the room. "Out!" he barked and looked around nervously.

Dan had no clue what was going on or what was about to unfold, but he and Carmen had little choice but to comply and move out the door.

Once they were clear of the cell door Dan didn't hesitate. He elbowed the man in the ribs and immediately followed that move up with a head butt that snapped the man's skull back. Dan wrestled the gun free from his grasp, then slammed the stock into the side of the man's face. Hard. The kidnapper crumpled to the ground unconscious.

It was difficult to tell what was going on in the darkness. A staccato burst of gunfire erupted somewhere in the jungle ahead, and those excited, high-pitched voices continued unabated. The situation was highly confusing, but one thing Dan did know is he didn't want to go in the direction of all that noise.

Clutching the gun in his right hand, he grabbed hold of Carmen's arm with his left hand and dragged her towards the protection of a thick pocket of jungle well away from the fight zone. Once they'd reached it, they dropped down to the ground and lay flat on their bellies.

Dan peered out between the leaves and really wished he had his trusty binoculars on him right now. He really couldn't make out much of anything in the darkness at this distance, but all he could do was guess that someone had attacked the kidnapper's camp. Who it was, he had no idea. He didn't know if it was the good guys or another group of bad guys with a score to settle. Now that they were free though, he didn't plan on going back to find out.

He turned to Carmen and whispered, "Let's get out of here."

They got to their feet and ran in a crouch. With no moon it was hard to see in the darkness. Dan didn't want to risk lighting their path with the flashlight, so the pair kept stumbling through the gloom, their faces continually being swatted by unseen branches.

Carmen fell to the ground with a thud beside him and he stopped to help her up. He tripped as well then and hit the dirt, his hand colliding with something that felt unnatural. He moved his hand along it and realized he was touching clothing, clothing that had a body inside of it.

Feeling his heart threatening to burst through his rib cage, Dan chanced using the flashlight and directed the beam on what had tripped them up. It was definitely a body. When he shone the light on the dead person's face, Dan couldn't help but gasp.

CHAPTER TEN

He could see it was Tyler. There was no doubt about it. He instinctively checked for a pulse, but the bullet wounds in his chest and head already told him Tyler was dead, and not recently either. His body was cold and bloated and it looked like he'd been dead for at least a day or more.

"Is that-" Carmen began.

"Yes."

Dan slumped to the ground feeling totally defeated. For a moment he couldn't think. What the hell was going on here? Tyler had obviously been killed long before the ransom payment was scheduled to be made. Why did they murder him? Was it because the money wasn't enough? Was that it? What was he going to tell John? *How* was he going to tell John that Tyler was dead?

He felt tears of frustration and grief well up in his eyes, but he forced the feeling aside. Instead, he snatched up the gun and got to his feet.

When he started walking back towards the kidnapper's camp in a huff, Carmen called out, "Where are you going, Dan?"

He looked back over his shoulder. "To shoot somebody."

He heard her race up beside him, where she latched onto his arm and forced him to stop.

"Shoot somebody? Are you mad?"

"Payback."

"You'll just end up in jail. And believe me, a Filipino prison is not a place a foreigner wants to be." She still gripped his arm tight. "If you go back there you might get yourself killed. Let's just get back to the city and sort this mess out as best we can."

Dan sighed heavily. He knew she was right. Him going back there shooting up the place wasn't going to solve anything. And it certainly wouldn't bring Tyler back.

"So what do we do with him?" he asked.

"You mean Tyler? We leave him where is for now until we call the police."

Dan hesitated a moment. "Do you think we can find our way back to the pickup?"

"That would mean backtracking through their camp," Carmen pointed out.

"I left the keys in it and I don't recall them taking them. Maybe we can skirt wide of their camp until we find the trail back to the basketball court."

"The kidnappers might have run off in that direction."

Dan shrugged. "Well how else are we gonna get back? It's not like there are some handy taxis around here. There's not much of anything around here."

When she eventually nodded, Dan took that as a signal that she agreed with him, so he set off in the general direction of the kidnapper's camp, but kept to the cover of the jungle as much as possible. As they drew nearer they could still hear voices, followed by the occasional crack of gunfire.

Dan went far left, dragging Carmen along with him, skirting well wide of the place. He figured if they kept moving in this general direction they would happen upon the trail that would take them back to John's pickup.

His sense of direction proved correct and soon they were cautiously making their way back to the basketball court in the middle of nowhere. The structure loomed up out of the darkness, still dully lit by that one weak bulb. In the distance Dan saw that the pickup's parking lights were still on, but now looked a little more yellow than white. The battery was being drained after so many hours.

Dan and Carmen remained in the cover of foliage as they surveyed the area, looking for any hint of movement or potential danger.

"Do you see anything?" Dan whispered.

"No."

"Let's keep moving."

They darted out from the cover of the jungle and hugged the edge of the basketball court. At the corner Dan paused again and made sure no one was lurking near the car. Feeling confident that nobody was about, he strode over to the pickup, opened the door, saw the keys were still in the ignition and switched off the parking lights.

"Just let the battery rest for a few minutes, then we'll see if it starts."

Carmen eyed the rifle in his hand. "Are you going to take that with you?"

"I think we'd better, just to be on the safe side."

After one last careful look around, Dan climbed in behind the wheel and turned the key. The old pickup struggled for a second, then rumbled to life, much to his relief. Once Carmen was in, he headed back out the way they'd come.

Dan didn't care about driving slowly down the mountain. He went as fast as he dared in the old car. On one hand he was in a hurry to get back to John, but on the other a part of him wanted to delay having to tell John about his brother.

When they reached the outskirts of Cebu city he was forced to take his foot off the gas, as there was traffic around despite the early hour.

In silence they drove the rest of the way to John's house. Dan cut the motor and hesitated before getting out. All the lights in the house were on, the front door was open and John immediately filled the frame, obviously having heard them pull up. He raced down the steps and over to the gate.

"What's been going on?" he demanded. "I've been trying to call you guys for hours. We've been worried sick. Agent Ramos was really concerned something bad had happened to you."

"Ramos?" Dan spat. "Where the hell is he?"

"He went looking for you." John glanced at Dan and Carmen, then at the pickup. "Tyler's not with you?"

Dan's heart sank. "No," is all he said for now.

"Come inside," John said and strode back into the house.

Carmen and Dan tailed him in. They found Joy in the living room looking tired and stressed.

"Ramos called me at around midnight asking if you two had gone to the drop off point," John explained. "He and his team had been delayed due to a bomb scare in one of the hotels. I told him you'd left hours ago and that I hadn't been able to contact you since eleven PM."

Dan let John say what he had to say. He wanted to know what the story with Ramos was, but anything to delay having to tell him the bad news was also welcome.

"I then remembered the GPS tracking device you'd put in the lining of the money bag, so Ramos said he was going to try and track your location with it. That was the last I heard from him." He collapsed on the couch next to his wife. "Now. Are you going to tell me what the hell's been going on all this time?"

Dan nodded and recounted their ordeal from the time they'd arrived at the basketball court in the middle of the jungle. He told them about how they were double crossed and taken prisoner, locked in the cell, and how they'd made their escape when, presumably now, Ramos and his team had arrived on the scene. Dan paused when he got up to the point of discovering Tyler's lifeless body.

"So you escaped and found your way back to the pickup?" John prompted Dan to go on.

Dan sucked in a deep breath and said, "Not quite." He glanced at Carmen, as if she might know of a way to break the news so it wouldn't be painful.

John sensed something was wrong. "What?" he demanded. "Do you know something about my brother?"

Dan decided he just had to tell him. There was no easy way.

"Not long after we escaped we found Tyler's body in the jungle. He'd been shot."

John looked at Dan and shook his head, his eyes betraying his disbelief. "You shouldn't say things like that, man. Not about my brother."

Carmen chimed in now. "Tyler's dead. I'm very sorry, John, but your brother is gone."

Dan said, "He'd been dead long before we ever even went there tonight. The kidnappers had no intention of letting him live. I don't know why." He threw up his hands in a useless gesture.

John got up and started pacing the room. He paused mid pace just long enough to look at Dan and say, "They shot him?" When Dan nodded he resumed his pacing. "And just dumped his body in the jungle like trash."

Dan had nothing to say to that. What could he say that would make his friend feel any better?

Carmen asked John, "Can I borrow your phone?" He pointed to it on the coffee table, so she picked it up and disappeared outside to make a call. After about ten minutes she returned. "I just spoke with Agent Ramos," she announced.

"What did he have to say for himself?" Dan wanted to know.

"It was him and his team that raided the kidnapper's camp. He's still working the scene up there. I told him briefly what happened tonight, and I also told him about Tyler. They're going to go search for his body and bring him back to Cebu. He also wants all of us to remain here. He's going to come see us when he's done up there and take our statements."

No one slept while they were waiting and there wasn't much conversation either. John hadn't burst into tears over the death of his brother or anything, but Dan could tell his friend was struggling to process what had happened.

When dawn broke Joy went into the kitchen and made everyone coffee. She included a plate of cookies on the tray. Everyone, including John, had a coffee, but no one was hungry enough to touch the cookies.

When the clock on the wall struck eight AM they heard a vehicle pull up outside the house. John leaped to his feet and went to take a look. "It's Agent Ramos," he called out, then went to greet the man from the NBI.

As the men entered the living room, Ramos was in the middle of offering John his sincerest condolences over the tragic loss of his younger brother. Ramos was accompanied by another agent who carried a clipboard and a pen, ready to take notes and statements. The man with the clipboard grabbed a dining room chair and took a seat, while Ramos seemed to prefer to remain standing.

"Tyler's remains have been located and transported to the morgue," Ramos went on in a surprisingly soothing tone. "We'll need you to go in and formally identify him." John nodded his assent. "We may yet conduct an autopsy. Although cause of death is quite obvious. Be assured we'll release him to you for internment as soon as we can."

For the next twenty minutes or so the agent interrogated both Dan and Carmen, making sure he had all the details of exactly what had unfolded up in the mountains. All the while the other agent scribbled furiously on his notepad with his pen. Dan had a few words to say about Ramos not informing them that he and his team couldn't be there on time, leaving them to fend for themselves. Ramos just seemed to shrug it off, which Dan thought was a very casual dismissal of their life and death predicament.

"You could have called us," Dan said.

"There was no time. We had an emergency situation."

"So did we," Dan snapped, struggling to control his anger.

Ramos literally waved him away with a flourish of his hand and turned his attention back to John.

"We've determined Tyler's time of death to be soon after you received the call with instructions for the ransom drop off." John looked momentarily stunned. "It seems they had no intention of ever exchanging your brother for the money. Do you have any idea why that would be?"

John shook his head. "None. I'm not even really sure I know what you're asking."

"It seems like they always intended to kill him no matter what amount of ransom money you paid. They wanted the money *and* they wanted Tyler dead. Can you think of any possible reason why these men would want your brother dead?"

Again John shook his head. "Maybe you can ask *them* why."

Ramos looked chagrined now. "I'm afraid that will be

impossible. All of them were killed in the raid."

"Even the one I knocked unconscious outside that concrete hut they used as a prison cell?" Dan asked.

Ramos turned to Dan and said rather sternly, "You did more than knock him unconscious."

"I killed him?" Dan was incredulous. "That's not possible. All I did was head butt him, take his gun and hit him in the face with the stock."

"And then shot him."

"I never shot him."

"No, he didn't," Carmen came to Dan's defence. "He just hit him, that's all, just like he said."

Ramos seemed to chew that over for a moment and eventually shrugged. "Well, someone shot him. I wouldn't really care if you did do it. One less piece of trash to deal with."

"Couldn't you have kept at least one of them alive so you could interrogate them?" John asked the agent.

"We weren't in a position to pick and choose. My men were taking heavy fire. One even sustained a leg wound, but he'll be okay. Should make a full recovery." He nodded at the note taker and headed for the door. "I'll be in touch. Call if you think of anything else that might prove useful." Ramos paused in the doorway and turned around. "Oh, and we recovered your money," he said to John. "It'll be released back to you in a day or so." He slipped a hand into his pocket then and withdrew two cell phones. He handed them to Dan. "I presume these are yours and Miss Mendoza's?"

And then the agents were gone.

Dan sat there trying to think of what to do next. In a way the case was closed. They'd failed. Tyler was dead. It wasn't what they wanted, but it was done. He was nowhere near satisfied though. Sure, the kidnappers had got theirs and were all dead too, but that still didn't answer the question why they killed Tyler, and seemed like they always planned to kill him.

Something wasn't making sense. Something just wasn't right. This didn't feel over, and it wouldn't until that question was answered.

"Will you tell Tyler's wife?" he heard Carmen ask John.

"I guess it should be me."

"I'll go with you."

"And me," Dan said.

He wanted to see Larissa again anyway, maybe ask a few probing questions.

CHAPTER ELEVEN

Knowing he had to get it out of the way, and Larissa needed to know what had happened to Tyler as soon as possible, the three headed off in Carmen's car to meet with Larissa and her family. John had called ahead saying they had some news, but didn't say what.

It wasn't something to be said over the phone.

John parked the car outside Larissa's parent's home in the subdivision and killed the motor. He sat there for a moment collecting his thoughts, sighed, then eventually got out.

The boy that had been staring at Dan the last time he was there was at the front door. Dan and Carmen trailed John inside the house. There was no sign of the angry little black dog today.

Dan remained standing, leaning against a wall. Carmen did the same. Larissa was sitting on the couch with her mother beside her. John took a seat adjacent to the two women and clasped his hands in his lap.

"There's no easy way to say this," he began, "I have some bad news." He took Larissa's small hand in his. Looking down at the floor as he said the dreaded words, John's hand started to shake. "Tyler's been murdered."

Dan watched for the reaction. There was a long pause of complete silence, then both Larissa and her mother started wailing in unison. There was a lot of noise that sounded like heartfelt grief, but streams of tears didn't flow as much as one would have expected with such an outpouring of emotion.

"I'm so sorry," John said, his own eyes welling up now.

John was genuinely grief stricken over the loss of his younger brother, but Dan wasn't convinced about Larissa and her mother. Something about their grief looked rehearsed, a predetermined scene being acted out.

He couldn't be sure though. It was just a hunch, a gut feeling he had. A former cop's intuition possibly.

Following his instincts, Dan took out his phone and opened up the voice recording app. He did it as discreetly as possible and kept the phone in his hands as if he were browsing something on the screen.

"Tyler!" Larissa suddenly wailed, then spoke something in Bisaya that Dan couldn't possibly understand. Her mother clung to her daughter and continued to wail as well. The little boy remained silent, just watching what was going on.

Dan had yet to meet Larissa's father. The man never seemed to be home. Maybe working, or overseas.

The mother started speaking in rapid Bisaya now. Larissa looked at her and screamed, "They shot him like an animal!" More wailing and crying and howling.

Dan smiled inwardly, but it was a grim smile. He leaned close to Carmen and whispered in her ear, "Go outside and call Ramos. Tell him he needs to get down here to speak to Larissa and her mother."

Carmen nodded, and he could tell by the look in her eyes that she'd heard the slip up too. Carmen went outside and crossed to the other side of the road before making the call. Meanwhile, Dan continued to record, just in case anything else of interest was said. Carmen came back into the house a few minutes later and simply nodded.

While she'd been away a group hug situation had developed, which involved Larissa, her mother and John all huddled together while they shared their grief.

It felt like a long wait between Carmen's phone call and when Agent Ramos arrived, but in fact it was only about twenty minutes. When he saw the NBI man pull up out front, Dan went out to meet him. Without saying a word he indicated for the big bald man to follow him down the road a little.

"Did you speak to Larissa and her family at all after you found out Tyler was dead?" Dan wanted to know.

"No. I knew John would probably break the news. I didn't plan to speak to them until later on today. Why?"

Dan played back the start of the recording and Agent Ramos nodded his understanding.

Dan said, "How did she know Tyler had been shot?"

"Exactly," the agent agreed. "Can you do me a favor and bring John outside. I want to speak to him privately for a minute without Larissa and her mother around."

Dan went back inside and asked John if he could have a word with him in private. John reluctantly left the grieving mother and daughter and was surprised when he laid eyes on Agent Ramos.

"What's going on?" he asked the big man.

"There have been some new developments that involve Tyler's wife and possibly her family as well. I just wanted to give you the heads up before I go in and start questioning them."

Agent Note Taker suddenly opened a car door and joined them in the street, and together they all filed into the small house. Now it felt really cramped inside.

All eyes were now on Ramos. The crying and wailing had ceased.

"I'm very sorry for your loss, Mrs Harvard," Ramos began in a gentle, but formal tone. "However, I do need to ask you a few questions and clear some things up."

Larissa looked nervously at her mother, then back at Ramos. She nodded.

He continued. "You've insisted all along that you didn't know who the kidnappers might be. Well, we've since run identification checks on all involved and it turns out one of them was your cousin, Alfredo. My team did some quick digging and found out that you were very close to him, but apparently Tyler had never met him. Are you still going to tell me that you knew nothing about this?"

Larissa shrugged and held up her hands. "Of course not. Why would Alfredo take my husband?"

"You tell me," Ramos said pointedly. He looked at Dan. "Play back your recording, please."

Dan did, then switched it off after everybody had heard Larissa's slip of the tongue.

"Mrs Harvard," Ramos said. "How did you know your husband had been shot? No one told you that."

Larissa sat there like a statue, stunned and not knowing what to say. The look on John's face now suggested he might be about to jump on top of the young woman and strangle her.

"It seems you haven't been truthful all along," Ramos went on, then added rather nonchalantly, "Your cousin is dead, by the way. I think you better come down to the station for a formal interrogation. We'll bring your mother along too."

CHAPTER TWELVE

Ten Days Later...

They had just had the funeral for Tyler Harvard. As expected, it had been a somber affair, and now everyone was gathered back at John and Joy's house for dinner and drinks. Some family had even travelled from America to attend, including the mother of Tyler and John.

After eating some more traditional Filipino food, Dan and Carmen grabbed a cold beer each and stepped outside to find some space and get some air.

Dan sipped his beer and looked up at a sky filled with converging storm clouds.

"Even though this is all wrapped up, it's hard to feel satisfied with the conclusion," he said. "What a total mess. I feel so sorry for John and the family."

"I know," Carmen agreed. She sipped some of her own beer. "I spoke with Agent Ramos a while ago. He told me both Larissa and her mother have now been formally charged with aiding and abetting a kidnapping and conspiracy to commit murder. Ramos seems confident he has enough evidence to convict them both."

Dan nodded, satisfied with that outcome at least.

"The mother still denies her involvement, despite the fact that Larissa claims it was her mother than came up with the plan and pressured her into going along with it?"

"Apparently," Carmen said. "But Ramos isn't concerned about getting a confession from the mother. He's very confident of getting a conviction against her."

"So all this was about greed," Dan said. "Money."

"Seems so. And the ransom money was only the small payout. A bonus. What they really wanted all along was to claim Tyler's life insurance policy. A cool one million US dollars." She looked at Dan. "That's an absolute fortune here in the Philippines."

"So much for true love," Dan spat, disgusted with the whole sordid affair. "According to John, Tyler loved Larissa to pieces. Everyone thought she felt the same way. Obviously not."

"Maybe she never did love him," Carmen mused. "Who can know for sure? I think John and Joy have something genuine though. I don't doubt that."

Visions of Tyler's lifeless body all alone up there in the jungle entered Dan's mind then. What a way to depart this world. So sad. What pained - and angered - him even more was that while Tyler was locked in that cell, all his thoughts would have been with his beloved wife, wishing he was with her, hoping she would find some way to help rescue him. But the complete opposite was true. That's fucked.

He sighed heavily and downed some more beer.

"Let's discuss something a little more pleasant," he said to Carmen and even managed a smile. "Apart from the obvious, there's something else I've been thinking about these past few days."

Now Carmen smiled. "And what would that be, Dan Mason?"

She sipped some beer, that familiar sparkle finally returning to her eyes.

"*You* deserve a reward for all your hard work on this," Dan said. "And *I'd* like to explore some of the more exotic places in your country."

"And?" she prompted.

"How about taking some time out and joining me on a tour of the Philippines? My gift to you."

"I don't know," she said, feigning a coy smile. "Travelling all alone with you. You might be tempted to take advantage of me."

Dan held up his hands. "I promise to behave."

"No, don't you dare do that."

I hope you enjoyed reading the second short book in the Dan Mason series. Keep an eye out for new titles in the series as they are released.

Also, please feel free to leave a review of Hostage. Honest reviews help us authors improve as storytellers, so we can craft the kind of books our readers really want to read. They also help keep us motivated to write the next one.

Thanks again for reading. Stay safe and stay happy.